# The Lunch Bowl

## Steve Boga

**High Noon Books**
Novato, California

The Lunch Bowl (Scoreboard)

Steve Boga
AR B.L.: 2.5
Points: 1.0                    UG

**Cover Design:** Jill Zwicky
**Interior Illustrations:** Ke Sneller

International Standard Book Number: 0-87879-992-3

10  09  08  07  06  05  04  03
15  14  13  12  11  10  9  8  7

You'll enjoy all the High Noon Books.
Write for a free full list of titles.

# Contents

# CHAPTER 1

## The New Kid

A lot of students watched the Lunch Bowl every day. They had time after lunch before the next class. Even some teachers came to watch. The football coach was there, too.

The Panthers broke from the huddle. The new kid stopped. He turned back to the quarterback. "Throw it out there. I will be open," he called.

"Right, kid," said Wolf. He was the quarterback. "That's what they all say."

Wolf looked over the defense guys. Pete Wilson was near the new kid. The new kid was pretty big. But Pete was the best corner back in the ninth grade. That new kid was wrong. He would not be open. No way.

Pete called out, "Hey, Wolf. Hurry up. Are we going to get in one more play before the bell rings?"

A kid on the sidelines called, "Don't worry. You've still got 10 minutes."

Pete waved at him. "OK, Ronnie."

Wolf started calling signals."One, two, three!"

The center was a big kid. His snap was perfect. It hit Wolf right in his hands. But the center was slow on his feet. He tried to block the kid in front of him. He missed. The rusher went by him.

Wolf was quickly in trouble. The kid rushing him was 6 feet 2 inches. He weighed 210 pounds. He was fast. Wolf was 5 feet 4 inches. He had a good arm. But he could not throw a football over a mountain.

Wolf faked to the left. Then to the right. Then another big kid closed in. Now four arms were waving in Wolf's face.

Should he give up? Or should he heave the ball down field? This was the Lunch Bowl. People were watching. Wolf heaved the ball.

He threw it as far as he could. He knew no

*The kid rushing him was 6 feet 2 inches.*

one would catch it. But at least he got to show how well he could throw.

The ball went so high, it looked like a punt coming down. But it went a long way.

The new kid ran straight at the corner back. It was Pete Wilson. Ten yards down field he slowed. Then he turned and raced right by Pete.

Ronnie, the kid on the sidelines, later said, "I've never seen anyone get by Pete like that. No one ever beats him. And that new kid beat him bad."

Coach Swill was watching. "The new kid is all alone," he said, "but the ball is way over his head."

The new kid looked back. He saw the ball

looping toward him. He put his head down and sprinted. Then something happened that no one had ever seen before. The new kid left the ground. But this wasn't a jump. It was a dive. There was a loud gasp from the fans.

"What's he doing?" asked Coach Swill.

"Call a doctor!" yelled Ronnie.

"He will be hurt," said Katie, a cute girl standing next to Ronnie.

Time seemed to slow down. The new kid hung in the air. His body was level with the ground now. He seemed to be stretched out on a pillow of air. He stuck out his hands. His body was straight as a knife.

The ball dropped down to meet his hands.

Fingers stretched out to meet the ball. The point of the ball hit his hands. And it stuck. It looked like a fly hitting fly paper.

Now the new kid had to come down. He tucked the ball under his arm. Then he tucked his head and turned it away from the ground. He hit on his shoulder and curled into a ball. Then he rolled all the way over and popped up on his feet.

He was OK. He was in the end zone. Touchdown!

For a moment, no one said anything. No one moved. No one blinked. They only stared.

Then the place got loud. The fans clapped and cheered. They had never cheered at the

Lunch Bowl before.

The players went running over to the new kid. A lot of them slapped him on the back.

Wolf ran the whole field. He slapped the new kid on the back, too. "Great catch! Nice tuck and roll!" he said. "Hey, what's your name, anyway?"

The new kid had a big smile on his face. "David Strong," he said.

"Good name," said the quarterback. "It works for me. I'm Wolf Ortez. Maybe we can do this again."

"Any time. You throw them. I'll catch them," said David.

"It's a deal," said Wolf.

The game was over. The bell had rung.

The crowd moved toward class. Wolf. walked off near Ronnie and Katie.

Ronnie raised his voice. "Hey, Wolf Man! Nice toss," he said.

"What's that new kid's name?" Katie asked.

"David Strong," said Wolf. "Is that perfect or what?"

"A very strong catch from David Strong," said Ronnie. He was using his deep voice. He liked to pretend he was a radio announcer.

Katie, Ronnie, and Wolf walked to class. While they talked, they all had their eyes on David up ahead.

# CHAPTER 2

## Sixth Period

It was sixth period after the Lunch Bowl. Ronnie was having a bad day. First he got a B- on a math paper. Then Katie said something that made him mad.

"You're not as smart as you think you are," she told him.

"Well, duh. Who is?" he said.

Ronnie laughed. But he felt bad. He was the class clown. He made people laugh. But it was easy to hurt his feelings.

He sat at his desk. He was talking to himself.

"OK, fine," he said. "So no one wants to talk to me. Then I'll just talk to myself."

"Go for it," Pete said. He wore a black bandanna on his head. Just like one of his NFL heroes.

"How about that new kid, eh, Pete?" Ronnie said. "That was quite a catch, huh?"

Pete did not look happy. "Stick to talking to yourself," said Pete.

"That catch was great. It was the best part of my day," said Ronnie.

"That's too bad for you," said Pete.

Ronnie turned back to his book. But then he

started thinking, "What would it be like to be David Strong? To trade places with him? Trade lives? Trade bodies? Yeah, I would make that deal. He can have my life. I'll take his," thought Ronnie.

Just then the door opened. In walked David. He had a slip for the teacher. He was coming into advanced math.

"Is he smart, too? said Ronnie in a loud voice. Everyone laughed. Laughs were what Ronnie lived for.

The teacher put David at the desk in front of Ronnie. Ronnie tapped David on the back.

"Hi. I'm Ronnie Shell," he said. "I kind of run things around here."

Three kids nearby laughed.

"David Strong," was the answer.

"I knew that. Hey, nice job out there at lunch," said Ronnie. "Do you do that often? Risk your life, I mean."

David shrugged. "It's not such a risk. You just have to know how to do it," he said.

Ronnie chuckled. "Teach me sometime. We can sell tickets," he said.

David said, "I get the feeling it's not a common play around here."

"Common? Nah. Around here we think all the bones in the body are important," Ronnie said.

## CHAPTER 3

## Friends

Ronnie and David became friends. They were tight for about six months. Some kids called them "the odd couple."

On Friday evenings, Ronnie would ride his bike over to David's house. David's parents were out a lot. They left David alone. He and Ronnie could do what they wanted.

They played basketball. David had his own court with lights. David would let Ronnie have 18 points. They would play to 24. David would still win.

Ronnie always joked about it. "You only win because you are bigger than I am. And stronger. And a better athlete. Stop me when you get sick to your stomach."

They laughed. David thought, "Ronnie makes me laugh more than anyone."

David also had his own weight room. They lifted weights for a while. But Ronnie hated lifting weights.

David said, "I hate it, too. But my dad makes me lift weights. 'Football players have to lift weights,' he tells me."

"That does it! I'm not going out for football," said Ronnie.

They laughed. Ronnie weighed about 110 pounds.

David said, "You know, I'm not that great in school. But my dad says I can go to a good college if I keep playing football," said David.

"Go for it," said Ronnie.

They liked to climb the hill behind David's house. The hill was covered with tall grass. They would slide down the hill on cardboard. They acted like race car drivers. David always went faster than Ronnie did.

Sometimes a night baseball game was on the radio. They liked to listen to it. They would lie on their cardboard and look up at the stars.

David would pretend he was a great

*They would slide down the hill on cardboard.*

baseball player. Ronnie called the game. He pretended he had a mike in his hand. He pretended millions of people could hear him.

"It's the bottom of the ninth inning," he would say. "The bases are loaded. And David Strong is stepping to the plate."

"Thank you. Thank you," said David. He raised his arms and smiled to the fake crowd.

Ronnie was into it now. "Every seat is full here. No one has left the park. Listen to those cheers!" he said.

"Yaaayyyy," said the boys, making crowd noises.

"Thank you. Thank you," said David to the crowd.

Ronnie went on. "The first pitch to Strong is strike one."

"Boo," went the boys.

"No problem. No problem," said David. He held his hand up. "I got two strikes left."

"The next pitch is . . . strike two. Right at the knees."

"Boo. Boo," went the crowd.

"It only takes one," David said. He held up his hand to calm the crowd.

"And here's the next pitch. Strong swings. He hits it a long ways. It's going . . . going . . . gone! A grand slam home run!"

The two boys played that game a lot. It was always the ninth inning. The bases were always loaded. David always won the game with a home run.

One warm night they were lying on cardboard up on the hill. A million stars shined above them. David asked Ronnie, "Do you know Katie Miles?"

Ronnie said, "Of course, I know her. I've known her since first grade."

David said, "I think she likes me."

Ronnie sat up. He felt sick to his stomach. "Why do you say that?" he asked.

"Someone told me. Besides, she smiles at me a lot," David said.

"Oh, she smiles at everybody. That's just the way she is. It's just a twitch, I think,"

Ronnie said.

David said, "I thought I might ask her out."

Now Ronnie's stomach really hurt. "I was going to ask her out, too," he said.

David sat up and looked at Ronnie. He was surprised. "You want to ask her out?" David said.

"So what?" Ronnie said. He sounded mad. David had never seen Ronnie get mad.

Ronnie went on, "What's the matter? I'm not good enough for her? You think only a big jock like you can ask her out?"

Now David was mad. "No," he said. "I didn't say that. But you have known Katie for ten years. What are you waiting for?"

"Don't rush me," said Ronnie.

# CHAPTER 4

## Katie

Ronnie never did ask Katie for a date. He was afraid she would say no. But David asked her out. She had hoped he would. They had fun. She thought he was nice. He thought she was pretty.

They started going steady. He gave her his letter sweater. She gave him a ring.

As the years passed, David was number one in baseball, basketball, and football.

But football was his best sport. He caught almost every ball thrown to him. He leaped. He dived. He always held on to the ball.

As a senior, David was the best football player in the state.

"His kind only comes along once every twenty years," said the coach.

In his first two years of high school, he caught 120 passes. David made some All-American teams.

College scouts would be coming to the Panther football games. They wanted to see David. They also wanted to take a look at Pete.

"What a country!" Pete said to David. "I get C's in school. But I can go to college for free. Why? Because I can play corner back. I make dudes drop balls."

## CHAPTER 5

## Radio Days

Ronnie's parents did not have much money. So Ronnie got a job.

He started working at a local radio station. It was called KRAG.

Ronnie just did odd jobs at first. He was now 18 years old. He still looked like a boy. But he had a man's voice.

They liked Ronnie's voice at the radio station. They let him go on the air.

Ronnie did an ad for toothpaste. He was the

voice of a beaver. "Brusha, brusha, brusha," he sang.

Then one day his boss gave him another job. "We want you to be the Voice of the Panthers," he said. "We want you to announce the Panther football games."

It was Ronnie's dream come true.

Ronnie bought a tape player. He practiced calling games. Then he listened to his own voice. He did this over and over.

"This is Ronnie Shell. Welcome to Panther football," he would say. It almost drove his parents crazy.

# CHAPTER 6

## Football Season

The Panthers' first game was against the Rams. The seats were filled an hour before the game.

Ronnie was nervous. He thought he might throw up. Except for that, he felt ready to do a good job.

Ronnie went on the air. His first words were, "Hi, everybody. This is Ronnie Shell. And this is Panther football on the air, KRAG, 99.1.

"This place is packed today. Three thousand fans. No empty seats. They are here to see David Strong do his thing. But they are also here to see this Panther team. Many think this team can go all the way.

"And here come the Panthers! And there's David Strong! He has added 20 pounds since last year. He's 6-foot-3-inches and 200 pounds. And it's all muscle. Some say he can bench press 100 pounds with his nose. Ha ha.

"The Panthers are wearing their new black and gold tops. Gold pants, black helmets. They look sharp.

"The Panthers will receive. They will go from my right to my left.

"And here we go! Pete Wilson takes the kick off. He heads straight up the middle. And he returns it to the 24 yard line."

The Panthers began to move the ball down the field.

This is how Ronnie called the last play of the drive:

"The Panthers have the ball at the 35. They come out of the huddle. David Strong is wide to the right. There's the hike. Ortez is back to pass. He looks left. He looks right. He lets it fly. It's a long one!

"He's got Strong all alone at the 5 yard line! But that pass will be over his head. Strong leaps. And – oh my! – David Strong makes a great catch. He rolls all the way over. And pops up on his feet! Touchdown Panthers!"

And so it went. Three touchdowns for David in the first game. Two in the second. Three more in the third game.

He broke records every week. No one in the state had ever caught more passes. Or gained more yards. Or scored more touchdowns.

Everyone was talking about him. He made the fans feel like winners.

You could hear David's name on TV. You could hear his name on radio. You could read about him in the newspapers.

When Ronnie filled his car with gas, the gas station owner loved to say, "Hey, Ronnie. How about that David Strong? Is he the best ever or what?"

"The best ever," Ronnie would say.

"Where is he going to school next year?" the man would ask.

"I hear he is going to skip college. He's going straight to the NFL."

They always laughed. But it made Ronnie feel sad. He didn't know what David was going to do. They never talked anymore.

Ronnie hardly ever talked with Katie either. Mostly he just watched her with David. It almost made him crazy. Sometimes he wondered if he could take it. "It's a good thing I have my radio job," he would say to himself. "It's the only thing I can do better than Strong."

# CHAPTER 7

## Panthers vs. Rams

After 5 games the Panthers had 5 wins. David Strong had 42 catches. He had 12 touchdowns. He was the talk of the state.

After 8 games, the Panthers were 8-0. After 10 games, they were 10-0. David Strong had 97 catches. It was the most in the nation.

Ronnie was getting better on the radio. Everybody knew who he was. But he was still alone. He had no girlfriend. He spent hours wishing he were David.

The Panther's last game was with the Rams. Both teams had 10 wins and no losses. The winner would be state champion.

The Rockville fans had never been this excited. Some people paid $100 for a ticket to the last game.

Ronnie woke up early on the morning of the game. It was raining hard. "Uh oh," he said.

At game time, the field was a swamp. The wind was blowing the rain to the side. It would be hard to score in such bad weather.

At half time, the score was Panthers 0, Rams 0. Ronnie said on the radio, "It is so muddy out there! I can't tell the players apart."

The Rams picked up a fumble in the 4th

quarter. They kicked a field goal. Now the score was Rams 3, Panthers 0.

The Panthers got the ball one last time. Two minutes were left in the game.

The quarterback threw short passes. The Panthers moved down to the Rams' 20 yard line. The clock showed 8 seconds left in the game.

Ronnie was at his best calling the last big play. "The Panthers are out of the huddle. David Strong comes to the right. Somebody muddy is the end on the left. But you can bet the quarterback won't throw to him.

"There's the hike. The quarterback is back to pass. He throws a long one!

"There's Strong wide open at the 10! Here

comes the pass. And the ball is . . . missed! And – oh my! – it lands right on top of a Rams player. The Rams have the ball!"

The game was over. The season was over. The final score was Rams 3, Panthers 0.

David hurt his knee in the Rams game. He could hardly walk the next day. He would miss basketball and baseball seasons.

He limped out of the doctor's office. A little kid ran up to him. "Will you sign my football?" asked the kid.

"All right," said David.

A man came up behind the kid. He had an ugly look on his face. "Don't give him that ball. He will just drop it," the man said to the kid.

# CHAPTER 8

## Aftermath

High school ended. Summer came. Ronnie left for college.

David decided to go to college at State. If he made the football team, college would be free.

One summer night Pete showed up at David's door. "Come for a ride with me," said Pete. They got into a shiny red car.

"Man, where did you get the ride?" David asked.

"It's a friend's car, man," said Pete. "It's on

*"Come for a ride with me," said Pete.*

loan. Come on."

They drove for a while. Then David said, "Let's go see if Katie wants to go for a ride."

They picked up Katie. The three of them sat in the front seat. Only Pete wore a seat belt.

Pete pulled up near a 7-Eleven store. "I will be right back," he said.

He went inside the store. A few minutes later he came running back. He slammed the door.

"What's the matter, Pete?" Katie asked.

"Nothing, man. Nothing at all," Pete said.

Pete stomped on the gas pedal. The tires squealed. They could smell rubber burn.

They headed out into the country. Pete was

racing the wind.

"Hey, Pete," said Katie. "Could you slow down a little?"

Pete kept driving fast. He said nothing.

Katie gripped David's arm. She was scared. David was a little scared, too. But he didn't want to show it.

Pete said, "Guess what? I learned something today."

"What's that?" David asked.

"No college wants me," said Pete. "They say I'm too small. Can you believe that, man? I lead the world in tackles. And I'm too small," Pete said. He sounded both sad and mad.

They were out in the country now. Trees

lined both sides of the road. The road was straight. Pete was doing 80 miles per hour.

"It's not that they don't want you," said David. He had to yell so Pete could hear him. The car was making so much noise.

"Well, they ain't giving me no money. That's like not wanting me," yelled Pete. Now he just sounded mad. And now he was going 85 miles per hour.

Katie dug her nails into David's arm. "Pete!" she started to say. But she stopped.

There were no more words. Only screams. And the sound of a car smashing into a deer. Then more screams. Then all was still.

# CHAPTER 9

## Grown Up

A few years later, Ronnie saw David on a street corner. "David Strong," said Ronnie.

"Yeah," said David.

Ronnie could tell David didn't know who he was. So he opened his arms and said, "Voice of the Panthers."

That did it. "Hey, Ronnie," David said.

They shook hands. "Boy, my first day back in town. And I run into you. What luck. Are you still living here?" asked Ronnie.

David nodded. "I teach P.E. at the high school. I also coach football," he said.

"That sounds like the perfect job for you. And how is Katie?" asked Ronnie.

David looked at Ronnie. "I guess you don't know what happened," said David.

Ronnie shook his head. "After I left, I never talked to anyone," he said.

"We were in a car crash," David said. He told Ronnie all about it.

"How is Katie?" Ronnie asked.

"She is doing better. She had to have some operations."

"What happened to Pete?" Ronnie asked.

"He wasn't hurt. He had his seat belt on.

But they arrested him. As it turns out, he stole that red car. Then he robbed that 7-Eleven store. He's still in jail," David said.

"Poor Pete. All he had was football. When that ended, he had nothing," Ronnie said.

David nodded. "You know, I'm out of football. I never got a scholarship. I never had a crack at the NFL. I walk with a limp. But in some ways, my life is better than ever."

"It makes sense. You are working with kids," said Ronnie.

"What are you doing now, Ronnie?" asked David.

"I'm still in radio. In Denver. I have my own talk show every day. I love it. It's great fun.

And one of the big networks wants me."

"Do you ever think about moving back here?" asked David.

"No, thanks. I got healthy when I moved away from here," Ronnie said.

"What do you mean?" asked David.

Ronnie paused. "I guess I can tell you now. All through high school, I was jealous of you."

"That's funny. I was jealous of you," David said.

"Me?" Ronnie laughed. "Why me? You had everything. No one was jealous of me. Except maybe a few midgets."

"You were smart and funny. I liked both those things," David said.

They talked for a while longer. Ronnie thought David seemed happy. David thought Ronnie looked fit and strong.

After a while, they shook hands and said good-bye. As they were walking away, Ronnie heard somebody behind him. It was a man talking to David. The man had a big smile on his face. He slapped David on the back. "Hey champ. How does the team look this year?"

Ronnie stopped and watched. David looked over at him. Then he laughed and gave Ronnie a thumbs up. Ronnie walked away. He was glad David was happy. But he was also glad that he hadn't traded places with him.